tiny, perfect things

Written by M.H. Clark

Illustrated by Madeline Kloepper

Today, we keep our eyes open for tiny, perfect things.

Like here, on the ground,
a yellow leaf that the wind blew down.

A spider's web that's caught the light.

A snail that climbed the fence last night.

See all the crows up in this tree?
I watch them and they watch me.

Here's a red bottle cap.

And a man with a beautiful feather in his hat.

And a flower growing through a sidewalk crack.

Look! Our shadows are holding hands.
They walk when we walk, and they stand
when we stand.

I see a cat on the steps.
And someone we know.

Let's wave hello!

Here's an apple, way up high.
Red against the blue, blue sky.

And now I see the pale, bright moon.

It's getting cold. Let's go home soon.

Around the corner, up the stairs.
The light is on; who's waiting there?

We found so many things today!
A leaf, a snail, a cat, some crows.

The world is full of wonders,
no matter where we go.

Can we go again tomorrow?

How many tiny perfect things can you find?

I wonder what we'll see.

The world is full of perfect things
when you come look with me.

COMPENDIUM.
live inspired

Written by: M.H. Clark

Illustrated by: Madeline Kloepper

Edited by: Ruth Austin

Art Directed and
Designed by: Jill Labieniec

Library of Congress Control Number: 2017958763 | ISBN: 978-1-946873-06-4

6th printing. Printed in China with soy inks on FSC®-Mix certified paper. A092012006

*Create
meaningful
moments
with gifts
that inspire.*

CONNECT WITH US
live-inspired.com | sayhello@compendiuminc.com

   @compendiumliveinspired
#compendiumliveinspired